DINNER
AT THE
LOST FACE

T. M. ADAIR

ISBN: 1-949219-02-9
ISBN-13: 978-1-949219-02-9

DINNER AT THE LOST FACE

"Please, would you turn down the music?" Winston asked the server.

"I'll ask," the server said. She dropped a menu in front of him, slid three more into the empty places at the table, and filled his water glass from a pitcher she picked off a neighboring table. Hopefully it was a fresh pitcher and not left over from other patrons.

Her name tag read Cassyopya. Winston wondered if that was just creative spelling, or did her parents think this was actually the correct spelling of Cassiopeia? Maybe her family was under the impression that

Cassyopya was the name of some African or Asian queen. She had a vaguely mixed ancestry look about her. He was probably treading on territory that was a little too personal, and he decided against asking about her name.

"Back in a few with some bread," Cassyopya said. She flipped her ponytail over her shoulder and swept back toward the entrance of the Lost Face Restaurant. He didn't have to ask whether the bread tonight was garlic bread or rosemary focaccia, given the smell of garlic hanging in the air.

"And another pitcher of water, please," Winston said. She waved without looking back. He decided to take that as an acknowledgement.

Winston sighed. Another night at the Lost Face Restaurant, another business dinner introducing customers to his new boss, Mick Evans, another few hours Winston would never get back.

So far, Mick had expected every customer dinner to be held at the Lost

Face. And Mick had ordered the same thing each time: a bacon swiss cheeseburger and fries. The Lost Face was mid-priced, so Winston supposed it did set a tone of I'm-here-to-work-not-entertain-you with their customers. But any number of restaurants would have fit that need.

Plus, the place was just too loud. They were in the back again tonight, as far from the noise of the bar televisions as possible. Winston had steered Cassyopya toward the table angled around the corner from the overhead speakers, though that area was darker than the main room. Even so, the eighties tracks played in that elevator-music style was inescapable. Like the night before last, he would probably have to ask several times to have it turned down.

On the other hand, it wasn't worth complaining to Mick about coming to the Lost Face, not when Winston was still trying to work out how involved in day-to-day work his new regional manager wanted to be.

This was Winston and Mick's third customer dinner in a week, with five more lined up and a handful left to schedule. Already Winston knew the menu by heart: burgers, steaks, asparagus, baked potatoes, sautéed mushrooms. Salads with trendy vegetables like yellow beets. House made chips, vinegars, and tartar sauce. Plus fried and grilled sandwich plates. Decent, but he'd rather not have another burger tonight, and a steak would be too much. No wonder the sales guys complained about their weight.

Winston didn't usually meet with their customers like this. His job was data analysis—Big Data, now that there was a sexy name for it—and usually he just gave the charts and graphs to the sales guys, whatever they asked him to put together. Although he might shake their customers' hands when they came into the office, he wasn't exactly on a first name basis with them. But he was on a first name basis with their results, their sales and ordering patterns, which ones would order and cancel, and how often a promised purchase fell through. He'd tried to arm Mick with a dossier on each customer and their habits, but Mick had thrown it on the chair near his desk and waved Winston off.

Was that a cover of an Elton John song playing? Honestly, why remake perfectly good music into almost unrecognizable instrumental versions? Every time a new song came on, he caught himself trying to identify they original.

Winston was pretty sure that one of the gentlemen joining them tonight ate vegan, so he probably ought to eat vegetarian himself, to keep the customer company. Luckily, the Lost Face menu had some decent vegetarian selections, left over from the original menu. It had started as a vegan place--hence the name, alluding to food without a face. The restaurant had changed hands, going from vegan to Irish pub to a steak and burger joint in just a couple years. Winston figured the vegetarian offerings must be popular, since they'd remained on the menu for so long.

Maybe a salad, or some stuffed portobellos? Winston didn't even consider the veggie burger—anyone who wanted a burger badly enough to expect nuts and soy to masquerade as meat probably shouldn't be a vegetarian. Tonight's veggie special was Quinoa Terrine. He liked to order from the specials, just to try something new, but the Quinoa Terrine wouldn't work. The modern fascination with ancient grains could have stayed ancient, as far as he was concerned. Quinoa always got stuck in his teeth, and how could he talk about customer service and shipments and sales promotion analysis with something stuck in his teeth?

*

Winston had finished his second glass of water and third slice of garlic bread by the time Mick showed up. Mick was dressed in a pair of dark jeans and a pale yellow button down shirt. The outfit made Winston's khakis, red dress shirt, and tie seem impossibly over-dressed.

Winston stood to shake Mick's hand, wishing he had known they were going to go casual tonight. With a place like The Lost Face, it was hard to tell whether to dress up or down.

Mick waved him back to his seat. Winston filled Mick's glass from the pitcher of water on the table, then refilled his own. He was definitely over his eight cup a day hydration plan, and he made a mental note to update his water consumption in his phone app later.

Mick settled into his chair. Or rather, his chair groaned and shifted to accommodate him. Mick wasn't heavy, so much as he was built wide and dense. He thumped his phone down on the table and ran a hand through his military-cut hair. A number one, which Winston could appreciate the simplicity of, but he found it a little too severe for himself.

"Torsen and Garrett didn't show yet, huh?" Mick looked around for a server. No luck.

Winston looked at the two empty chairs at the table as if they would turn up some explanation. "No, not yet."

Mick laughed. "Fifty bucks says they won't show at all."

"It's a dinner meeting, they're probably caught in traffic."

"Nah, they're not coming. C'mon, take my bet."

"I don't bet."

"I bet you don't."

Winston took another sip of his water. How could Mick be so certain Torsen and Garrett weren't coming? Had he talked to their office? No, if he had, he would know for sure if they had cancelled.

"You see what I did there?" Mick prodded.

"I got it," Winston said. "How long do you want to wait for them?" He took out his phone and thumbed through the calendar. "I don't see a cancellation."

"Let's just eat," Mick said. "If they show, they show. But they won't. And for the record, I was funny and you should have laughed." He leaned forward. "It's polite. Loosen up a little."

"I talked to the office at Supply Solutions," Winston said. "I don't see why the office would agree to the dinner if they weren't going to send someone."

Cassyopya came around the corner to their table and set a draft beer in front of Mick. "You want the usual?"

"Bacon swiss cheeseburger and fries," Mick nodded.

Cassyopya turned to Winston. She was chewing gum, and he could smell the sweet bubblegum flavor, even over the garlic in the air. It was probably not sanitary for restaurant staff to be chewing gum. He looked back down at his menu. He'd been planning to order vegetarian just to be polite to the Supply Solutions guys, but Mick seemed so certain that they wouldn't show.

"I'd like the tuna melt, please," he finally said. "With fries." If Torsen and Garrett were going to be late, it served them right if he had tuna breath when they arrived. And he didn't want to laugh at Mick's jokes. The whole idea irritated him. Winston took his job seriously. How would it look if their customers showed up and he and Mick were laughing and joking around? Especially this customer—not one of their best, but a broker that had the potential to do a lot more business with them.

Of course, according to Mick, they probably weren't coming, so what did it matter anyway?

"Gotcha." Cassyopya grabbed the water pitcher from their table and she headed back to the front of the restaurant. "Back with a refill in a bit."

Winston didn't like how the evening was proceeding. He'd been here with Mick a couple of times, but they'd never had the same server twice. The guy must come here a lot, if Cassyopya knew his regular order. How many times did you have to come to a restaurant in order to have a usual? And what if you didn't show up again for a while? Did you still have a usual order, or was it more of a use-it-or-lose-it kind of thing?

"All right, what makes you think that Torsen and Garrett aren't coming?" he asked.

Mick grinned. "You know as well as I do, maybe better."

"No, I don't think so."

"You said it in their brief: 38% returns after promotions, and 29% late orders. Highly opportunistic about new items, order but don't take delivery, huge market share and we have hardly any business with them."

Winston thought about that while he

picked at his napkin. "You actually read the reports I give you?"

Mick rolled his eyes. "Of course. I mean, you could stop with all the color charts and graphs. A crappy customer is a crappy customer no matter how you color it. Color print costs money, you know. And Supply Solutions is a crappy customer no matter how you print it."

Winston shook his head. "The sales guys like the charts."

"No, they don't. They use them for target practice at Donny's."

Winston blinked and looked up from his napkin. Donny's was across town, almost out of town, really. Nowhere near the office. "Donny's pool hall?"

Mick nodded. "They drink and throw darts there on Friday nights."

"They throw darts at my charts." The elevator-style music was playing an adaptation of an original by Pink Floyd. Surreal. Winston wished he too were somewhere else.

"Right." Mick picked up the last piece

of garlic bread and inhaled it in one bite.

"Really? They throw darts?"

"Really."

Winston took a swig of his water, frowned, and put it back down. Mick must spend time with the sales guys between customer dinners with Winston. If the guys were throwing darts at his reports, they'd be making fun of him, too. They called him Weenie Winston behind his back, and who knew what other names they might have for him?

"Hey, don't let it bother you," Mick said. "At least they're looking at your reports. I mean, from a distance."

Winston wished he could just get up and walk away. The whole situation bugged him. Their clients were thirty-three minutes late, and his new boss was hearing who knows what about him from his coworkers. Probably because they didn't really consider themselves his coworkers. To them, he was just Weenie Winston with the goofy graphs.

"Maybe I'll go up to the bar and get a beer."

"Really? I thought you didn't drink."

"I don't drink much," Winston corrected him.

"I'll get it." Mick pulled his phone out and pressed a couple buttons.

"You have the waitress on speed dial."

Mick nodded. "Hey Cassie, Mick. Can you bring me another, and one for my friend, too? Also, can you turn the music down?" He ended the call and looked over at Winston. "You don't have a favorite beer or anything, do you?"

∗

Cassyopya brought their plates. Between the two of them, there were probably enough fries for four people. She winked at them, a big exaggerated wink that showed off what looked to Winston like a complicated mixture of brown eye shadows. "Kitchen dumped too many fries into the fryer so I brought them all," she said.

Mick snorted. "I like fries," he said.

"I know," she said.

"Ok, you're the data geek," Mick said after Cassyopya dropped off a bucket containing ketchup, barbeque sauce, malt vinegar, and horseradish sauce. "You tell me how many times these guys have stood us up?"

"Dinners or sales meetings?" Winston asked. "I guess I didn't know that they had a track record like that." He peeked beneath the top layer of his sandwich, which was nicely toasted. He was happy to see the cheese was still bubbly. A positive sign, piping hot food. "I could ask their account rep, I guess."

"Then let's try this one," Mick mumbled around a mouthful of burger. "How many account reps have we assigned to Supply Solutions in the last three years?"

Winston thought for a moment, running through their sales staff in his head. He hadn't really considered it before, but Supply Solutions had been assigned a number of different reps. None for very long, though. "Five?"

"Close. Six. Every six months your former boss reprimanded the salesperson assigned to this account, docked their commissions for not getting anywhere, and then assigned the account to whomever was the top salesperson at the time. Did results improve?"

That was an easy one. Winston shook his head while chewing. Sales with Supply Solutions were worse, not better.

"Right. In fact, overall sales are down across all accounts. Do you know why?"

Ah, well, just when he had been on a run of one good answer for three questions, here was another stumper. Something else he couldn't answer with all his market data. But the sales guys kept asking him for more detailed information on the items in their line-up, so he could guess.

"We have the wrong product mix?" he tried.

"No. We have the wrong strategy."

Winston guessed that could be true. Strategy wasn't really his mandate. He was the data guy. Sales strategy was the regional director's problem. Mick's problem.

"What's your strategy going to be?" he asked Mick, who was already done with his burger and texting or something on his phone.

"Well for one thing, we're not going to pursue Supply Solutions' account at all. As far as I'm concerned, they're dead to us. Pounding our heads against that wall is killing our results."

Winston raised his eyebrows. "They're the biggest broker in the region. They serve fully a third of the market. That's a lot of potential to forego."

"Forego, schmorego." Mick dismissed the idea with a wave of his hand, just barely missing hitting his beer in the process. "You know as well as I do that that we don't make any money off them."

"They contribute to the top line…" Winston knew that was a weak response and stopped himself. Why did he feel a need to defend the account? They didn't mean anything to him. "Well, top line looks good, or at least not bad, but after accounting for cancellations, the profit isn't good at all. They actually cost us money."

Cassyopya showed up with another basket of garlic bread and a third beer for Mick. Still no water, but Winston forgot to ask until after she had left.

"Exactly. Three years, six sales people, and the numbers look worse than ever—and all because of this one account," Mick said. "I really like this garlic bread."

"Well," Winston picked at his fries. "That account doesn't look good but it doesn't impact the others."

"Sure it does."

"How?"

"It's the old race to second place."

Winston just glanced at Mick. Mick had started in on his third beer and reached across the table to get at some of Winston's fries.

"Crazy little thing called human nature," Mick joked. "You don't mind if I have some of these?"

"No, go ahead." Winston pushed the plate toward Mick. "What's this crazy thing?"

Mick angled his head toward the speaker. "Crazy Little Thing Called? The song?"

"Oh." Winston thought the song sounded familiar but couldn't place it. Of course, all the music sounded familiar when transformed into elevator-csque tracks. Was that even legal? Was there a bad composer somewhere stealing bands' work and making it, well, unintelligible?

"Anyway, who wants to be top salesperson?" Mick asked. "Who wants to get Supply Solutions' account next? No one, that's who. Why try to make better numbers when all you get for your effort is the punishment of a crap account?"

"Are you serious?" Winston asked. "The sales team is holding back on possible sales, in order to avoid being assigned to Supply Solutions?"

"Yep. Get a couple quarters of good commissions and, bam! You're saddled with an account where your contact won't even call you back. All you get for doing a great job is the crappiest job ever. And we're done with that nonsense. I'm serious. Supply Solutions is out."

"I didn't realize," Winston said. "I should have correlated their sales over time and by assignment. I didn't think—"

"Or you could have just hung out with the sales guys for a while and they might have given you the idea, too. It's not all about correlations and market data, you know."

Winston could have kicked himself. He picked at his fries some more. They were starting to get cold and now they were a little soggy, greasy. He was supposed to think bigger, he was supposed to be able to see the big picture, prove it with data.

"What if Torsen and Garrett had shown up tonight? Was this their last chance?" He shoved the last of his fries over to Mick.

"I didn't think they'd show. They haven't shown up for a meeting in the last couple years. But if they had, I was going to tell them that we were canceling their account."

"I suppose I deserve to be called Weenie, since my analysis of that account was so far off the mark."

"Ah, don't be so hard on yourself, Weenie," Mick laughed, draining his beer. "Want another?"

No." The bit in the bottom of his beer was warm, and he probably wouldn't even finish that. "I've got to drive."

"Luckily I live just across the street, so I walked." Mick grinned and fiddled with his phone.

"Across the street? That's a motel." Winston frowned.

"Yep, I'm staying at the motel while I'm in town. A couple more weeks, anyway, then I'm going to the North-East region."

"I thought you were our new regional manager. Who's moving into town next?"

"No one," Mick grinned. "Because you're the new regional manager. Good luck with the sales guys, and stop letting them call you Weenie."

Cassyopya showed up with the check, and Mick signed it.

"Cassie, when are you guys going to get with the future and let me pay with my phone," he asked her.

"When the veggie burgers grow wings," she quipped as she headed back toward the bar. "See you tomorrow?"

"See you tomorrow," he agreed, and turned back to Winston. "You're awfully quiet. Don't want the job? It's a good one. And I've already fixed your biggest problem by dumping Supply Solutions. You can email them the good news tomorrow."

"I don't have any sales experience," Winston said. He didn't even have much experience with his own office's sales team.

"That's fine," Mick said. "I already knew that. I don't need a sales person in charge. That's the problem we already had. None of the sales team can give up on this account. They hate Supply Solutions but they're too emotionally attached to it to just drop the account in the toilet where it belongs. I need someone in charge who can look at a bigger picture."

But Winston knew he hadn't been looking at the big picture. How could Mick be so calm about this? Winston's palms had started to sweat and he couldn't even hear the music over the blood rushing in his ears. Was he having a panic attack? Winston wasn't sure he knew what a panic attack was, but maybe he was having one.

"The sales team doesn't like me very much," Winston said.

"Doesn't matter," Mick shrugged. "You just need to get out and interact with them a bit. Go on some sales calls with them. Ask each of them to take you to meet their favorite client, then ask them to take you to their best client. You'll learn enough, and they'll warm up to you."

Winston nodded. That didn't sound so bad.

"Ask people a bit about themselves, get them talking," Mick advised as he pushed away from the table. "Cassie, for example."

"What about her?"

"You know that's not her name, right?"

Winston shook his head.

"The Lost Face owner has some concern about people stalking his staff. So, they have a box full of name tags and none of them wear their own name. Sometimes you'll come in here and she won't be Cassyopya anymore either. She'll be Mitzi or Debra or something."

"Because the owner doesn't want people stalking his staff."

"Right."

"But you've been calling and texting her all evening. Obviously, you know who she really is."

"Right again," Mick laughed. "Once you get to know people, it's a whole different story. That can be your first assignment. Get to know Cassie."

Winston was conscious of the silence in the dining area as he followed Mick toward the bar and the front door. Finally, the music had been turned not just down but off.

The idea of being regional manager seemed unreal to Winston. Could he really manage a group of people that called him names behind his back? He pushed the worry to the back of his mind to consider later. It was odd to hear bits of other conversations at tables they passed. What was in a name anyway? What did he care what they called him?

And now he was oddly curious. He would have to come back to the Lost Face, if only to find out what was Cassyopya's lost name.

MORE BY THIS AUTHOR

If you enjoyed *Dinner at the Lost Face*, you might also like *Cure for the Sleeping Woman*, another contemporary story.

Contemporary Short Fiction:

Cure for the Sleeping Woman

Effie Gennings likes her history orderly and her small town museum ship-shape. Even if she and the museum are basically invisible to everyone. But when a mummy dubbed the Sleeping Woman is unearthed from a local bog, and displayed in the museum's facility until the University can take charge, people take notice. Even Eddie Adams, whose fears drive him to face to face with the Sleeping Woman. A contemporary short story available in e-book, paperback, and large print paperback.

Speculative & Science Fiction:

Plug & I (Offworlder #1)

Far out on the edge of Strikken-controlled space, a human who calls himself Plug joins the short-term crew of a mining ship. The Deep Sky Company hauler DSC18 is piloted by a slow-rider, a species naturally able to connect into the machine and operate the ship via thought. This slow-rider has led hundreds of humans over his years at the helm. But what's a pilot do when the genetically modified Plug wants to change things up? A short story.

Plug 2.0 (Offworlder #2)

Gilberto isn't used to his new implants. He doubts himself, his decisions to throw a stalker off the DSC-18 mining hauler, and his ability to become more than he was originally designed to be. Now, the CEO of Darling Investigations, Inc. has shown up, looking for his grandson, the stalker that Gilberto and Ryde expelled from the ship months ago. A novella.

The Gresmingas Incident (Offworlder #3)

Gilberto is under increasing pressure to prove himself, both to the clinic back home and to the Company that owns the hauler. But to prove himself threatens both Willa and Ryde. Even if he can find a way to make all three of them happy, what's he to do when his simple demonstration of control over the mining ship goes horribly wrong? A novella.

Gin-Nee's Dance Bar

Jacqui needs Doc, her brother's med tech and best friend, to explain how it's possible for her brother's memory to be returning. It shouldn't be possible after re-education. Doc works at Gin-Nee's Dance Bar, and clubbing isn't Jacqui's thing, but her friend Katt comes along. Inside is a scene Jacqui never expected--

no wonder Katt was so willing to come when Jacqui called! A sci-fi short story.

Library Friends

Celia loves books and loves the library...and most of the time she loves the friends she makes there, too. Her fondest wish is to take big kid books home to read. But the librarian, Mrs. Immer, doesn't seem to be on Celia's side, and sometimes, neither does Celia's friend Clara. A speculative short story.

Pick Up On Slisker

A story set on the planet Slisker, where pure bred Sliskers, humans, and human-Slisker hybrids co-exist uneasily...Walton chose this pick up from the freelance options the Agency gave him because of the soft target. The human lived in a suburb on the edge of the forest, but without her Slisker mate. No matter his experience, no matter how many agents he'd trained, Walton preferred an easy pick up with little potential for violence. But his target isn't alone, and his pick up takes a surprise turn for the dangerous. A novella.

Poetry by Tracy May Adair:

Stars Crawl Out From Their Caves
A full-length volume of poetry available in e-book and in paper.

Apples, Figs, Pomegranates
A chapbook first published in 1993 and now available in e-book only

Blog:

You can follow Tracy May Adair on her site at adairauthor.com where she blogs about fiction and poetry. Links to publications in on-line journals, poems, and audio clips of the author reading some of her poems can also be found at her site.

www.ingramcontent.com/pod-product-compliance
Lightning Source LLC
Chambersburg PA
CBHW050919120626
46552CB00004B/1656